MARTEE DARES TO DANCE

WRITTEN BY

HARRY SHUM JR & SHELBY RABARA

ILLUSTRATED BY

BIANCA AUSTRIA

Martee woke up to the sounds of happy hip-hop beats. The smell of coconut bubuto led him to the kitchen.

"Good morning, Martee!" Lola chimed, her words mingling with the sizzling of frying eggs. "So what was this doing in the trash?"

"I'm not going to the dance, Lola. I have to work on my planet presentation." Martee did not want to talk about the dance.

Lola pursed her lips. "You love to dance! School is important, but so is having fun."

Lola weaved her arms in a figure eight while her knees swiveled in and out. "You remember the Butterfly, right? Dance with me, apo ko!"

Martee's palms started to sweat. He remembered the last time he danced at school.

He quickly grabbed his lunch and was out the door.

The whole school was abuzz with excitement for the Halloween dance. Martee and Yasmine sat at their usual table.

Bagels WITH Scream Cheese!

Vampire Veinilla Ice Cream!

BOORITOS!

"I was thinking of dressing up as Saturn!" Yasmine giggled as she unwrapped the corn husk from her tamale. "But, Saturn has 146 moons, and that's a lot of moons to glue to my costume. What about you?"

Martee unwrapped the banana leaf from his tamale. "Oh, I'm not going."

"Why not?" Yasmine asked.

"Um, well . . . I don't think I . . ." Martee didn't want to tell Yasmine he was afraid he would be made fun of again.

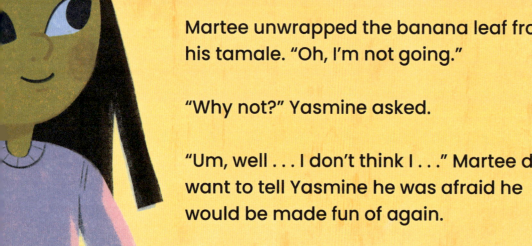

Halloween Dance!

Yasmine smiled and handed Martee her tamale. "Tamale tradsies? Don't worry, Martee, you still have time to think about it."

Martee's nerves calmed as they swapped lunches.

That night, Martee couldn't sleep thinking about the dance. A soft knock at the door brought him back to Earth.

"I was thinking about DJ'ing tomorrow's dance. You know you love my sick beats!" Lola winked.

Martee sighed and hid under the covers.

"Sleep on it, sweetheart. You might feel different in the morning."

Martee shut his eyes and whispered, "I never want to be laughed at again."

The lights of the galaxy on his ceiling started to swirl faster and faster.

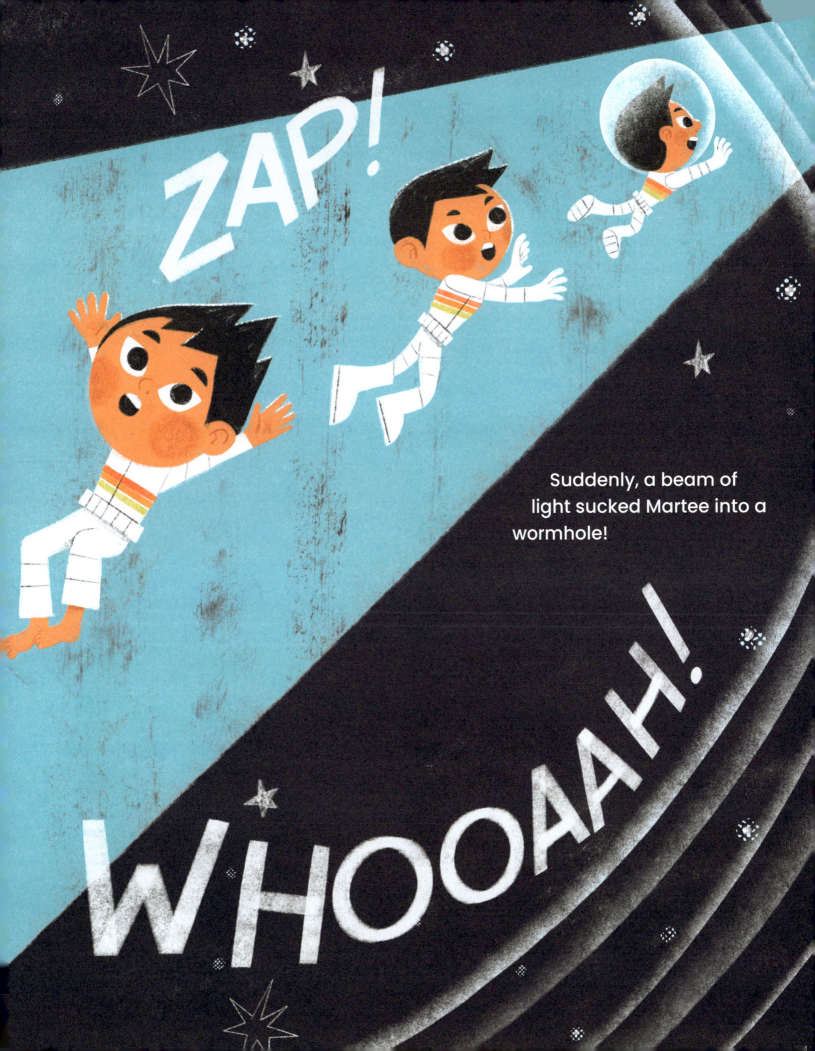

Suddenly, a beam of light sucked Martee into a wormhole!

Martee landed hard on his feet.
His heart pounded. "Where am I?"

"Wait a second. Huge volcano.
Red sand. No way . . . I'm on Mars!"

Martee pumped his arms in excitement when he noticed another dust cloud getting closer and closer.

"AAAAAHHHH!" Martee yelled.

It was a Martian copying Martee's every move!

"A Martian? In a hat?" Martee said.

The Martian winked at Martee then threw its hat in the air like a frisbee.

In a split second, the hat spun and stretched into a spaceship.

Martee and the Martian soared through the solar system. Winds jostled their spaceship as a kaleidoscope of clouds whirled all around them. "Swirling storms . . . that's Jupiter!" Martee realized.

"Swirl swirl!" the Martian said while circling its arms toward each other. The spaceship hovered still. The Martian did it again and looked at Martee.

Martee wasn't exactly sure what the Martian wanted him to do. He slowly copied the Martian's moves. The spaceship rattled. As he circled each arm toward the other, the spaceship propelled forward.

"Swirl swirl!" Martee repeated as he circled his arms and the spaceship took off into the glittering darkness.

SWIRL SWIRL!

The spaceship dodged Saturn and its many moons. Martee beamed with delight. "Yasmine was right! Saturn does have 146 moons!"

"Dodge dodge!" said the Martian, moving side to side.

"Dodge dodge!" repeated Martee as he leaned to the left and then to the right.

DODGE!

DODGE!

The spaceship went faster and faster. Martee's laugh grew louder and louder.

Geysers of ice suddenly shot up in front of their spaceship.

"Geysers! That's Triton, one of Neptune's moons!" Martee exclaimed.

"Whoosh whoosh!" the Martian said, shooting both arms above his head.

Before it even finished its second move, Martee was already in sync with the Martian.

The spaceship took a sharp turn as Martee and the Martian danced their way toward the Sun.

"That's Venus!" Martee blurted. More confident than ever, Martee jumped from foot to foot. "Hot hot!"

The Martian followed Martee, both of them dancing together.

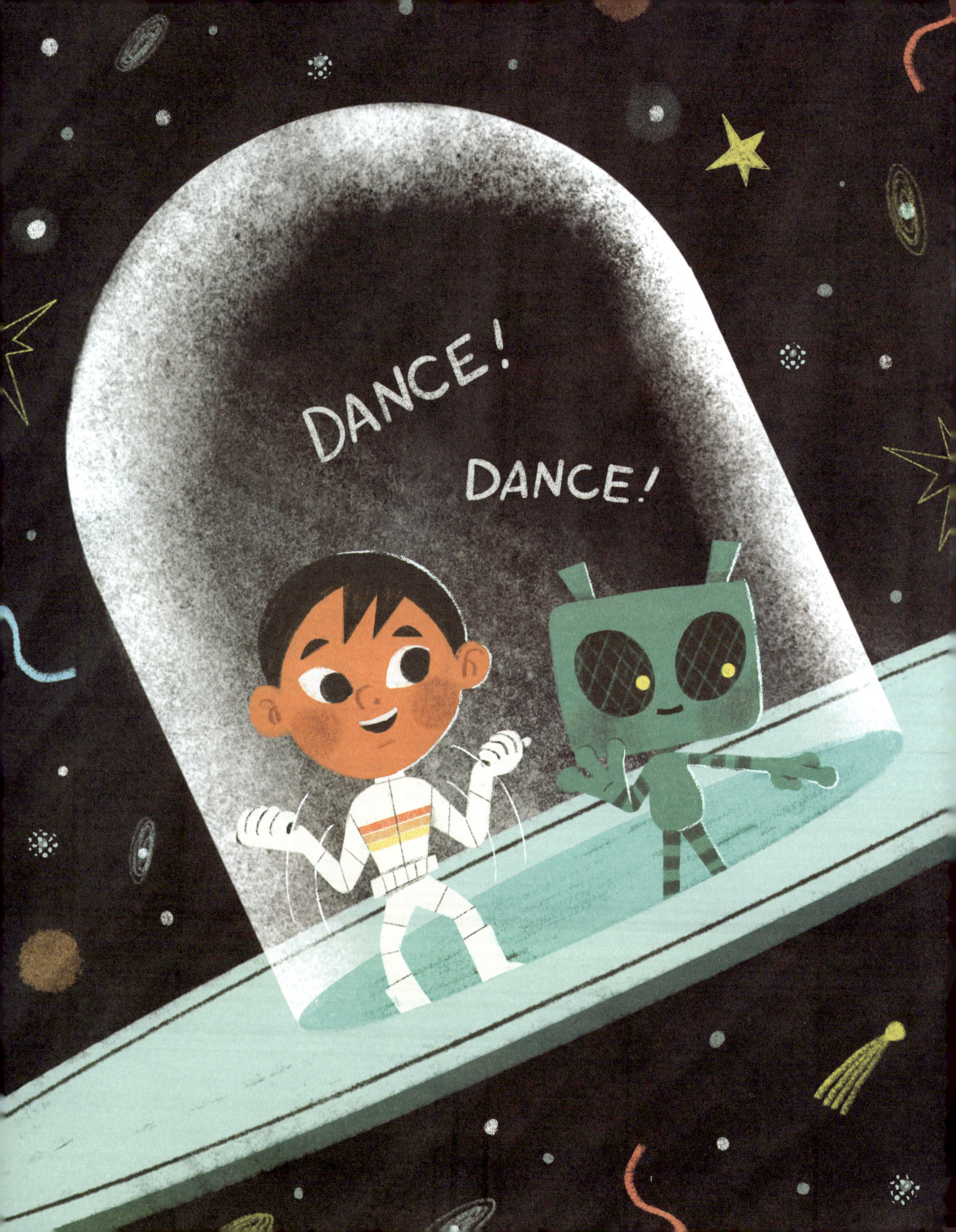
DANCE!
DANCE!

"What about the other planets?" Martee asked.

The Martian pointed at Earth. "Dance dance!" the Martian said as it weaved its arms and legs dancing the Butterfly.

Martee danced along, "Dance dance!"

Sunlight streamed through the blinds. "Swirl swirl, dodge dodge, whoosh whoosh." Martee mumbled in his sleep.

As his feet hit the floor, he hopped back and forth saying, "Hot hot!"

HOT!

HOT!

Martee sprang out of his room.

"Lola, I had the craziest dream! I met a Martian, and we explored all these planets in this spaceship hat, and the Martian showed me the coolest moves."

Martee stumbled over his words, talking a mile a minute.

"Look, he even danced the Butterfly!"

"Wooow, look at you go, so confident. You're ready for the dance," replied Lola.

"Martee, that is one awesome spacesuit!" Yasmine exclaimed as she wobbled into the dance.

Martee's palms immediately started to sweat. He stepped onto the dance floor and told himself, "You got this, Martee."

"Swirl swirl.

Dodge dodge.

Whoosh whoosh.

Hot hot.

Dance dance!"

To Xia, may you always be your true self
and never stop exploring the unknown.

— Harry and Shelby

For my little brother,
who courageously and beautifully
embraces his true self. Keep shining!
– Bianca

Martee Dares to Dance is first published by Gloo Books 2024.

Written by Harry Shum Jr and Shelby Rabara

Illustrated by Bianca Austria

The illustrations in this book were rendered in digital medium.

For more information or to order books, please visit www.gloobooks.com or contact us at contact@gloobooks.com.

Follow us @gloobooks.

ISBN: 9781962351041

Printed in China.